First published in the United States, Great Britain, Canada, Australia and New
Zealand in 2009 by North-South Books Inc., an imprint of NordSüd Verlag AG,
CH-8005 Zürich, Switzerland.
Distributed in the United States by North-South Books Inc., New York 10001.
Printed in USA by CG Book Printing, North Mankato, MN 56003, March 2010.

Library of Congress Cataloging-in-Publication Data is available.
ISBN: 978-0-7358-2255-9 (trade edition).
10 9 8 7 6 5 4 3

www.northsouth.com

I WANT A DOG!

By Helga Bansch

NorthSouth
New York / London

Lisa loved dogs.

BiG dogs, small dogs, SHORT dogs,
TALL dogs, shaggy-haired dogs,
curly-haired dogs, any kind of dog.

"I want a dog," she said twenty-one times a day.

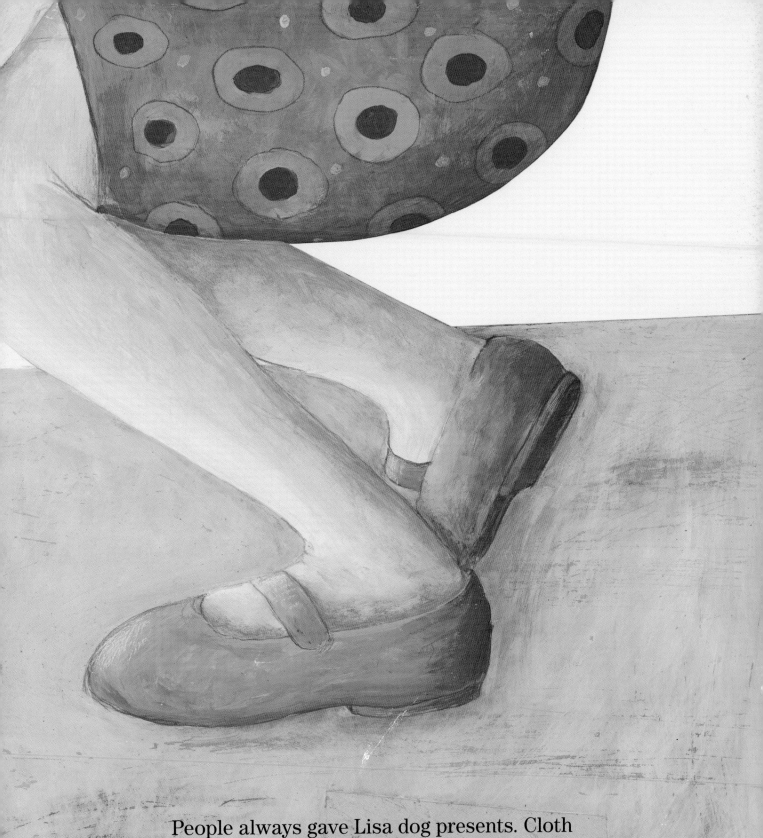

People always gave Lisa dog presents. Cloth dogs, wooden dogs, knitted dogs, china dogs, but never a real dog.

"Our apartment is too small for a dog," said Mom and Dad.

"A dog couldn't go to the mountains with us," said Dad.

"Dogs love the mountains," said Lisa.

"Our apartment is still too small," said Dad.

"A dog couldn't go to the beach with us," said Mom.

"Dogs love the beach," said Lisa.

"Our apartment is still too small," said Mom.

Every night Lisa had dog dreams.

Lisa tried to be really good—maybe that
would change her parents' minds.
"I will be as good as gold," she said.

"That will be lovely," said Mom. "But our
apartment is still too small for a dog."

"Then I will be **TRULY TERRIBLE,**"
said Lisa.

"Still too small," said Dad.

For her birthday, Lisa got a doll, two books, three
dog jigsaw puzzles, a china cat, and a computer game.
But still no dog.

"I need a better plan," said Lisa.

The next day, she hung signs all over the park.

WANTED
DOG TO BORROW
WALKING   BRUSHING
PETTING   PLAYING
YOUR PET NEEDS A PAL

SEE LISA.
DOG'S BEST FRIEND
77 OAK STREET APT 3

Two days later, the doorbell rang. There was an old man with a rather fat dachshund.

"I'm Mr. Lewis," he said. "And this is Rollo." He pointed to the dog. "Does Lisa-Who-Wants-to-Borrow-a-Dog live here?"

Lisa's parents were very surprised, but they invited Mr. Lewis in. Rollo waddled in behind.

"I'm getting too old to give Rollo the exercise he needs," Mr. Lewis explained. "He's getting fat. He needs someone young to walk him and to play with him."

"What a great dog!" said Lisa.

"What a great idea!" said Mom and Dad.

Rollo was
SMART

and
CLEVER

and
PLAYFUL

and a bit of a
Tease.

Lisa loved him right from the start.

Now Mom and Dad are happy. The apartment is just the right size for a dog who doesn't live there.

Mr. Lewis is happy. He has someone to walk his dog.

Rollo is happy. He has a new friend.

And Lisa is very happy. Finally she has a dog!